A VERY SCRAGGLY CHRISTMAS TREE

Story by Christie Pippen
Illustrations by Shirley V. Beckes

Raintree Publishers
Milwaukee

For: David, Jennifer, Dorothy,
Pauline, Bobbie, Rachel, Joan,
Steve, Nathan, Tema, Mike,
Kay, Suzanne, Carole, and Rosebud.
— **S.B.**

2 3 4 5 6 7 8 9   92 91 90 89

Library of Congress Number: 88-18564

Library of Congress Cataloging-in-Publication-Data

Pippen, Christie.
   A very scraggly Christmas tree.

   Summary: A sad and lonely tree high on a mountain is transformed on a stormy Christmas Eve, drawing children from a nearby village for a joyful holiday celebration.
   [1. Trees—Fiction. 2. Christmas trees—Fiction. 3. Christmas—Fiction] I. Beckes, Shirley V., ill. II. Title.
PZ7.P64225Ve   1988 [Fic]   88-18564
ISBN 0-8172-2654-7

Once on a very high mountaintop there lived two huge, shapely Christmas trees. Their lives were spent very happily. They held their limbs just right so the wind would feel good when it blew through their beautiful needles. They laughed and played with the birds that made homes for their babies in the branches.

The trees felt blessed, because all around them, they had their own baby Christmas trees. In fact, they had so many little Christmas trees that some grew faster than others. That meant that some were destined to live in the shade of their taller and older brothers and sisters. One of these unfortunate little fellows was Cedric, a very scraggly Christmas tree.

Cedric was very unhappy because he was so little and ugly. He had no shape at all. In fact, his trunk wasn't even as large as one of the smallest of his parents' limbs.

Cedric cried a lot and asked his parents, "Why don't I grow? I want to be just like you. I want to be tall and have a beautiful shape so someone will want me to be their Christmas tree.

His mother looked down at her tiny, ugly son and said, "I'm sorry son, you will never be any different, for without the sun you can never grow."

Oh, how sad this made little Cedric.

Then one day—as the days began to grow shorter and much, much colder—Cedric heard a strange noise in the forest. He recognized the sound of people, and they were walking closer and closer. He heard them talking about his family. At first, Cedric thought that it must be someone from the village out looking for a Christmas tree.

But Cedric was very wrong.

The people Cedric heard were greedy Christmas tree salesmen. They would go into the forest and chop down every Christmas tree they could find, leaving none for the poor villagers. Then they would take the trees into the cities and sell them at a very high price.

That meant that the villagers also had to buy the trees, since none could be found after the men left. Some people, who couldn't afford the high prices, had to do without a tree.

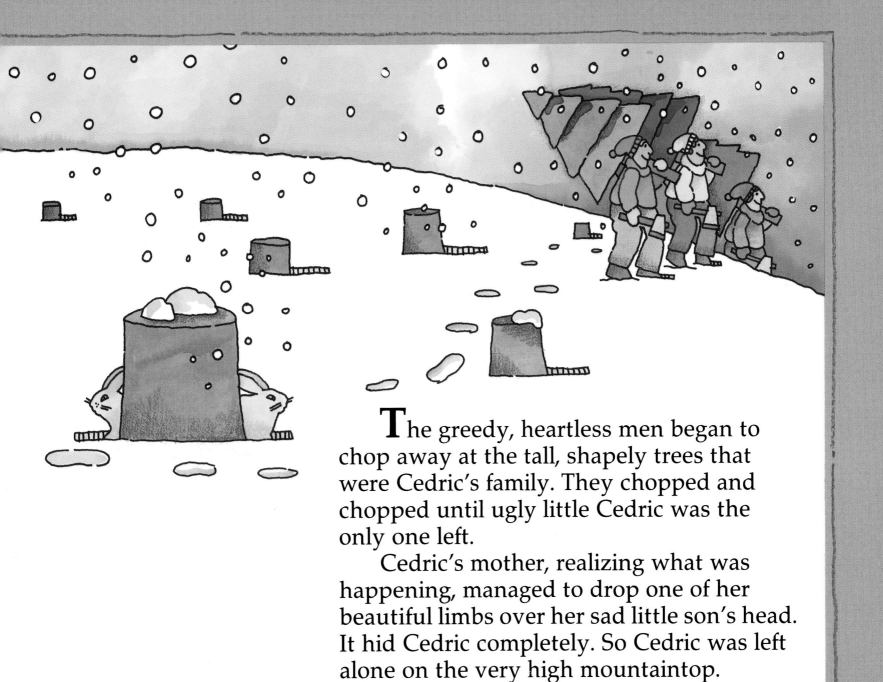

The greedy, heartless men began to chop away at the tall, shapely trees that were Cedric's family. They chopped and chopped until ugly little Cedric was the only one left.

Cedric's mother, realizing what was happening, managed to drop one of her beautiful limbs over her sad little son's head. It hid Cedric completely. So Cedric was left alone on the very high mountaintop.

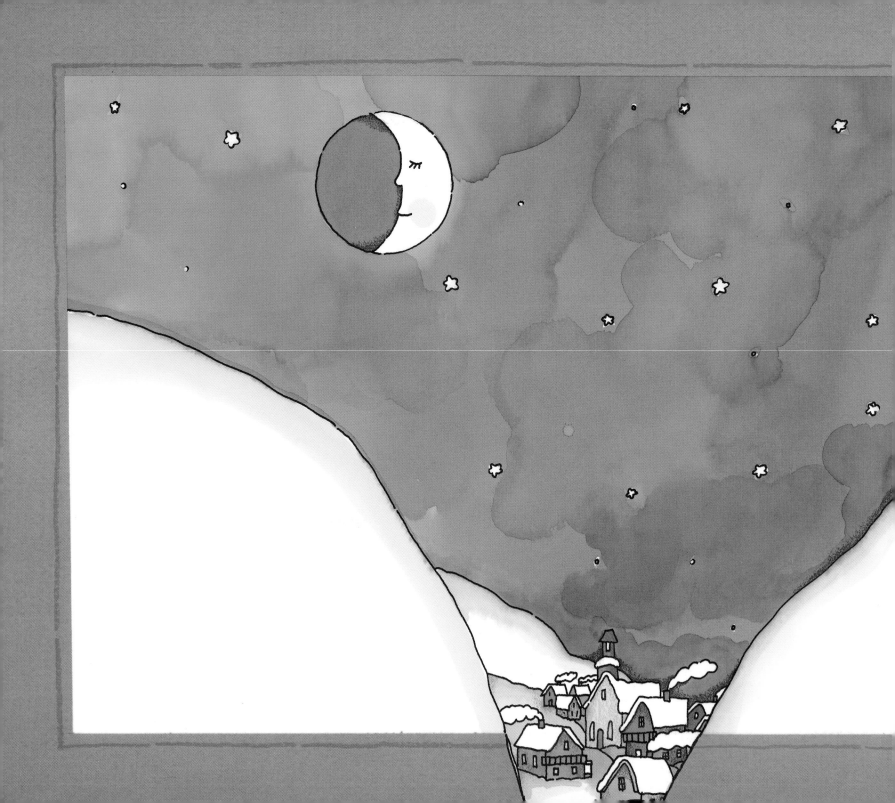

Although he was extremely sad and lonely, Cedric realized for the first time in his life that he could actually feel and see the sun. He knew that someday he would grow tall and beautiful. But even this thought didn't lessen the pain he felt in his heart.

So through the cold and windy days and nights little Cedric stood all alone on the mountaintop. His only comfort was the little village he could now see in the valley below.

The village Cedric saw was a poor village.
So, the Christmas tree salesmen didn't bother to
stop there with their trees. They went on to large
cities. This left the poor village without a single
Christmas tree, and there were none in the forests.

The village children began to worry and cry,
because they knew that without Christmas trees
and their lights, Santa wouldn't see their tiny
village. Their parents told them that nothing
could be done about Santa Claus, but Christmas
wouldn't be completely canceled. They made
plans for a Christmas program, and for the
children to go from house to house singing carols.

Well, Christmas came and with it a huge snowstorm. The children's program was canceled, but the children refused to give up their caroling.

Cedric listened carefully and could hear their singing. He thought it was beautiful, and he realized it was Christmas Eve.

Then the wind gave a mighty puff and much to Cedric's surprise, he, too, was singing . . . louder and louder. The stronger the wind blew, the louder Cedric sang, and the worse the storm grew.

Suddenly Cedric heard another sound. "Jingle, jingle." Then he saw a bright red glow above him. Cedric was a little frightened until he saw a jolly-looking old man and eight tiny reindeer land right beside him.

Santa looked at Cedric and said, "Was I glad to hear you singing. The storm had become so bad that I thought I was lost. I couldn't see a single light on a tree.

Cedric quickly told Santa about the greedy men who took all the beautiful Christmas trees from the forests. He also told Santa how his mother had hidden him.

Santa listened carefully to all Cedric told him. Then he rubbed his beard, and a twinkle came into his eyes.

25

Then, suddenly, Santa was in his sleigh flying up, up, up. He flew up above the storm, and just as suddenly, he came back down. In his hand, he carried a big, bright, shining star. He put the star on Cedric's head. Then he reached into his pocket and sprinkled Cedric with stardust. This made Cedric glow all over. He looked down at himself and saw that he was no longer ugly. In fact, he was very beautiful. Santa placed gifts and lots of toys around Cedric and then, as quick as a wink, he was gone.

The children were out caroling in the terrible stormy night and were amazed at the sight on the mountaintop. They ran to get their parents, and everyone stared at the beautiful, glowing tree on the mountain. The bright star beckoned to the village people to come to the mountaintop. As they traveled up the mountainside, they heard singing coming from the top. It was "Joy to the World," so they joined in.

To everyone's surprise, below the huge, bright star stood a tiny Christmas tree. They all agreed it was the most beautiful tree they had ever seen.

Cedric felt ten feet tall—seeing all the happiness in the children's faces and the joy in their parents'.

The village people and Cedric never forgot that Christmas. From then on, they always protected Cedric from the salesmen. And now, every Christmas is celebrated around Cedric.

April 15, 1988, was Christie Pippen Day in Crossett, Arkansas. That was the day that the city honored Christie for her contribution to her town and her school upon the publication of her book, *A Very Scraggly Christmas Tree.*

Christie was eleven years old, in the sixth grade at Daniel Middle School, when she wrote her story, which was sponsored by her teacher, Gail Thomas. Her favorite subjects are math and English. When Christie grows up, she wants to become a teacher. Christie enjoys reading, drawing, working puzzles, and ... jumping on the trampoline. Christie and her family, which includes two brothers, B.J. and Mike, live outside of Crossett near Lake Georgia Pacific.

Christie drew on her own experience to write about Cedric the Christmas tree. Her family, and her father's family, had always cut their trees from the area where they lived. Recently, however, all the trees in the woods near Christie's house were cut down. And that is when Cedric and his story were born.

The twenty honorable-mention winners in the **Raintree Publish-A-Book Contest** were: April Maria Burke, Old Town, Maine; Christine Debelak, Cleveland, Ohio; Aaron M. Eddy, Crossett, Arkansas; Tanisha Feacher, Homestead A.F.B., Florida; Brandon Geist, Schwenksville, Pennsylvania; Neal Kappenberg, North Bellmore, New York; Meegan Kelso, Coeur d'Alene, Idaho; Erin Mailath, Onalaska, Wisconsin; Olivia Julian Mendez, Richmond, California; Arnie Niekamp, Findlay, Ohio; Rebecca Papp, Hacienda Heights, California; Angela Rodrigues, San Lorenzo, California; Kirsten Ruckdeschel, Webster Groves, Missouri; Hannah Schneider, Washington, D.C.; Tres Sisson, Kaufman, Texas; Jenny Stalica, Buffalo, New York; Kenneth E. Stice, Des Arc, Arkansas; Kelley Tuggle, Largo, Florida; Regan Marie Valdes, Tampa, Florida; Scott Yoshikawa, San Jose, California.

Artist Shirley V. Beckes has been illustrating children's books for fifteen years. She graduated from Columbus College of Art and Design. Shirley, her husband David, and her daughter Jennifer live in the Milwaukee area, where she and David have their studio, Beckes Design/ Illustration.

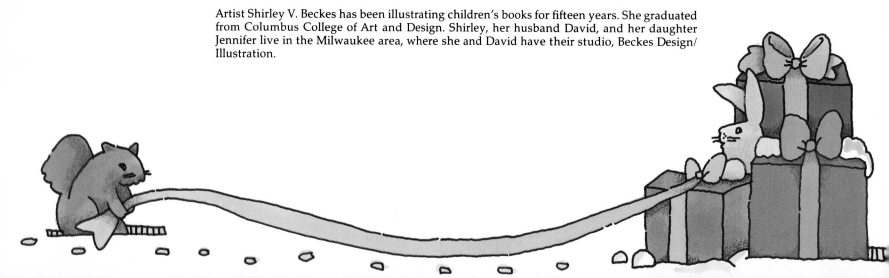